DEADBEARD

MATTHEW CASH

This book is dedicated to the mighty brethren of The Badass Bearded Nation, and especially to those that star in this, and to David R Shires at

www.theimagedesigns.com

Cheers one and all,

Keep it hairy xxx

Foreword

This book is a nail-biting, gripping story.

It has a unique and interesting twist in the way that Matty has captured the characters based on the members of The Badass Beard Nation. I enjoyed reading the story from start to finish. This is a book that you will read again and again as it's such a mind-fuck due to the unique writing style.

It's a pleasure to be featured in it as Detective McMillan.

Thank you to the Author for including me in this immense story.

I look forward to much more from him.

Dead beard, the enemy of the Badass Beard Nation.

Robert McMillan, CEO THE BADASS BEARDED NATION

Author's Foreword

A few weeks back I received an invite to become a member of a Facebook group collecting the world's finest specimens of bearded individuals under one roof.

David R Shires invited me as he had obviously taken note that I, for large parts of the year, am a hairy bastard. I like facial hair, once it was just an excuse to be lazy and the fact that I hate the way my skin feels after a wet shave and the fact that shaving uncovers the multitude of my gluttonous chins.

I'm a natural born twiddler, nothing filthy honest, and I am always messing with something, mostly hair twiddling.

So it saves me from having to walk around with my hands down my pants twiddling on my tangerine candyfloss.

It is more acceptable in public to twiddle with one's beard hair than pubic.

However, saying that I haven't grown this bush on my face purely to keep my hands out of my crotch like a filthy damn pervert, I actually like the way it looks.

I am not a hipster. Even though I adore the image.

So I joined this wonderful hairy community with its beard products, advice, support and not to mention incredible members and fundraising achievements.

It felt good to be part of something with like-minded individuals.

As a joke and part challenge to myself I made the comment 'maybe I should write a beard horror story.' Usually, for me, this is the spark that ignites a plot inside my head and almost out of nowhere this bizarre hair-hating psychopath was born. I had to ask myself and answer all the questions about this character and why he is what he is.

I chose to use real people from the community as characters as a gesture of goodwill and to help spread the good word that Robert McMillan is preaching.

It's not just about the beards; it's about community and coming together in numbers to achieve bigger and brighter things.

Let me introduce you to the nemesis of The Badass Bearded Nation.

DEADBEARD.

Matty-Bob June 2016

PROLOGUE

Detective Robert McMillan crushed his third can of energy drink in a hand the size of a bear's paw and tossed it into the back of his car. He wiped the residue of the sweet drink from his lips and into his bushy red beard, *fuck it, at least it'll smell different.*

He sped around the corner and immediately slammed on the brakes when he saw the ambulance parked haphazardly in front of the house. He jumped out of the car and amongst the melee outside the couple's house he sought out the authorities.

A couple of patrolmen kept a worried and eager crowd of Press and morbid onlookers at bay, he started towards them.

McMillan flashed his identification at the patrolmen and immediately those members of the Press who caught sight of his I.D were at him like a bunch of ravenous puppies.

"Is it true that it's another DeadBeard?" A crazy-haired woman screeched at him.

McMillan ignored the question and made towards the house just as the front door was kicked open and paramedics rushed someone out on a stretcher. They were so fast but he had seen it all before, male victim, almost always alive, head wrapped up in a thick wad of gauze and bandages, straws in his mouth and nostrils so he could breathe, paramedics doing the best they could until they could get him into the ambulance and to the hospital.

As if by clockwork, the second victim of the night was led from the house, the punchline in DeadBeard's horrific prank. Usually, the girlfriend, wife, once the mother. A young skinny blonde, hair matted down with blood, eyes wild with terrified agony, her husband's moustache and beard, not to mention the skin it grew from, surgically attached to her screaming face.

1

Great Bald Eagle may sound like a really cool name for a Native American. You picture maybe ruddied skin, far off wistful eyes, someone who can find you water or skin a snake, long plaited black hair decorated with trinkets and beads. Something that may automatically earn respect. But when you look like I do, with the parents I had, you can kiss goodbye to any kind of credibility straight away.

I don't know what the fuck drugs my parents were on in the late seventies, I am surprised that they can even remember my conception, let alone have both been physically healthy enough to reproduce. But I blame the copious amounts of washing detergent or maybe fucking hair removal cream that my fat old skunk of a cunt mother stuffed inside herself, cut with the lowest grades of whatever she could afford to snort reality away.

I was a long baby, not a big baby, a *long* baby. I've seen nasty horrid blurred photographs, that look like they should be in black and white and have Classified stamped across them with a big red stamp.

I resembled something from an abortion clinic in Roswell. Bulbous, completely bald head, protruding bulging eyes and a nose that was more beak than nose. I was Mr Burns from The Simpsons, only less yellow with one crazy, lazy eye.

The night of my conception, the spiritual manifestation of no other than infamous Red Indian Geronimo possessed my father's near-comatose drug-addled carcass and proceeded to rut my mother like a horny injun. My father insisted that this was indeed the case, as at the time, to have had the number of drugs necessary for him to participate in any carnal act with the woman who would be my mother, would have been more than his body could contain.

So somehow, whilst my dad was off floating on the astral plane after eating my mum's fungal infection, out of his fucking tree, Geronimo shouted his own name and filled my dad's boots. And my mother.

All that is completely beside the point, however, the point is that they called me Great Bald Eagle, due to the fact that mum was ridden by the frisky spirit of massive bighorn, and the fact I was born without a single hair. Anywhere.

It would have been more believable for them to have told me I was the result of an alien abduction, the first human-alien hybrid.

I grew up with constant ridicule. The name, my name, and my apparent ancestry should have helped me become more noble. That's what my dad had reckoned. It just helped me get my head cracked like the abnormal egg it resembles.

I was the school punch bag, the subject of everyone's jokes, even the sad loner kids who were usually bullied were treated like royalty if I was around. My weird appearance was the main focus of the jibes, my stupid, stupid name secondary.

I even once and I hate myself for even considering it at the time, I once told everyone to call me Jeebee, you know to try and be cool, instead of Great Bald Eagle, or GBE. Or Alien. That just gave the cunts a new line to use, so Heebie-Jeebies was another thing they would sling.

I survived school, but at a very young age, something had snapped inside my head. I bore an irrational hatred for hair. When I was a kid I used to wear those cargo shorts that had like a million pockets, and my prized possession was my Swiss Army Knife. In toy shops, whilst my parents kept the security guards paranoid with their dishevelled vagrant exteriors and the fact that they shoplifted everything, I would find the section where the plastic dolls were and cut all the hair off. It made me feel better about myself.

As I grew older, this bizarre hatred for hair grew more intense, I bought razors and stole people's pets from their gardens and tried my best to make them as bald as I could. But it wasn't enough, this burning hatred that could only be sated by destroying hair wanted more. My teenage years saw the onset of hormones and the start of my sexual interests.

The joy I had for cutting the hair off of toy dolls metamorphosed into wanting women who were completely hairless, not just down there either

Fetish sites with PVC were a huge turn on, slick, shiny skin, but almost always too much hair. I had no chance of sexual relationships, despite everything in that department being physically normal, in fact, my penis was quite big and, I had been told by people online, very handsome. But what's the good of having the world's best cock if it's attached to something that should have been in The X Files?

I needed something to take out my rage on.

My first victim was a woman; I thought it would help with my sexual inadequacy and frustrations.

I usually cover up quite a lot, such a scrawny gangly thing like me got more than enough attention, and I'd hide beneath long sleeves and hoods.

I saw her at the cinema, I used to frequent there a lot, the darkness was perfect at hiding abnormalities, and she was with her friend, a man. She had the most stunning hair I had ever seen, long thick ringlets that were dyed baby pink, which flowed over her naked shoulders like a strawberry milkshake. I wanted to burn it.

The weather was nice, a sunny evening, after the film, she took the canal towpath home and I followed.

Old derelict factories which were long forgotten and buried beneath loathsome graffiti were the perfect place for my first date.

It was simple; I followed her, found my opportunity and dragged her into the nearest factory.

Knocking her out proved a lot harder than I thought it would be, I don't know if I was doing it wrong or she was resilient or what, but the bitch would not stay down. In the end, I smacked her really hard with a brick.

The first thing I did, as any normal sexually deprived and depraved, psychopath would do, was take off all of her clothes and lose my virginity. It was alright, nothing special and I wish I had cut her hair off first, or possibly during, but I was a beginner.

As soon as I'd satisfied myself with sex, I pulled out my scissors and cut every last piece of hair from her body. Unfortunately for me, and maybe fortunately for her, she only had hair on her head. When I had removed her hair, I took the bottle of lighter fluid from my coat and set fire to it. The smell was divine. I wish I had burnt her hair whilst I raped her.

I didn't kill her; I just left her where she was, with a haircut like GI Jane or Ripley in Alien3.

I did this a few times, it was fun. The papers called me Edward Scissorhands, after the Tim Burton film.

Sometimes I'd mix it up a little, attempt to cut it off whilst I had my wicked way, but it was too tricky.

Like everything else it became mundane and just not enough to satisfy that little demon inside of me. Hair grew back, that was the problem. To destroy someone's hair by shaving it off against their will was, even though obviously very traumatic for the victim as for all they knew I may kill them, only temporary. I wanted; I needed to destroy any chance of them ever growing it back. Killing wasn't the right way to go; I wanted them to endure the same mockery that I had. I wanted them to suffer for having something I hadn't.

The hours people spend on their hair disgusts me.

Thousands of hours wasted preening, millions spent on products, lotions and potions. It was after an argument with my parents about my so-called ancestry that an idea surfaced.

What, in all the old cowboy films, are the Native American Indians famous for, aside from talking funny, feathers and shit, and firing bows and arrows at horse-drawn wagons? That's right, scalping.

I researched the process, marvelled over illustrations and even old photographs of the damage my forefathers were capable of.

In the last decade or so I began to notice an influx of preening, plucking, follicly obsessed men. This masculine side of the species was becoming just as narcissistic as the females.

Big bushy beards like sailors, rabbis and lumberjacks were puffing up out of the chins of men everywhere. Matching glasses that were purely for decoration perched atop pierced noses. Behold the birth of the present day hipster.

It infuriated me that these men wouldn't just be happy and grateful for their gift of being able to grow beautiful lustrous hair, oh no, they had to pander and prattle about with their own sets of lotions and potions and straighteners and curlers. Gels, sprays, putties, cream, wax, glue, hair mustard for fuck sake! And now beard oils, beard balms, on beards that were modelled on those warriors the Vikings, who would have washed their whiskers in the intestinal juices of their enemies whilst they still fought for their last breath! It sickened me, and so I upped my game.

I had a new plan; I was going to bring back the torturous slaughtering side of my rumoured forefathers, with my own special twist. I became the unknown horror to the badass bearded nation, a name they would cry out in the night as their fingers clutched reassuringly to the grizzled forests on their chins.

I became DeadBeard.

2

McMillan pushed the key into the lock as quietly as he could. Christ knew what time it was, he had texted Emma a few hours previous saying he was going to be late. The way he was going he'd end up like your stereotypical detective, living alone and living on a diet of alcohol and fast food. Daring not to even breathe, he entered the black hallway and closed the door without making a sound. He turned slowly and felt around in the darkness for the hook to hang his keys.

"Hello."

"Shitting Jesus!" McMillan shrieked as his wife appeared out of nowhere, his hand flew up in the air like a spasticated Thunderbird puppet and the keys went flying. "What the flaming hell you doing lurking about in the dark?"

"I like the dark," Emma said switching a standing lamp on, he saw she was wearing one of his Marvel T-shirts as a nightie, it immediately gave him the horn. She pursed her lips together and said, "Quack." It was a silly little joke they had, she would do the infamous pouty duck face and say quack, and as he was considerably taller than her, he would duck down and kiss her.

He grabbed at her waist and planted a big kiss on her face. "I'm glad I didn't wake you up."

"Who says you didn't?" Emma said one foot on the bottom step of the stairs.

McMillan raised his finger, "I just know these things, and I'm a detective after all."

Emma twisted her mouth up, "defective more like."

"Plus you've still got your glasses on, which means you've probably been reading Christ knows what by fuck knows who needed a wee so came downstairs and happened to be on the way back when I sneak in."

"Hmm, smart arse." She said pushing said glasses up her nose.

"Seriously what time is it?" McMillan asked fumbling in his pockets for his mobile phone.

"Last time I checked it was half eleven."

"Shit, really? I'm sorry babe; we had another fucking CuntBeard attack."

Emma grunted with disapproval, "I saw on the news. I saw you on the news. Don't you think you should, you know?" She circled her finger around her mouth.

"What? Get rid of the beard?" McMillan asked, genuinely offended.

Emma nodded, she knew it meant a lot to him but it was just hair.

"It's not just hair you know," he began.

"Oh please," Emma interrupted.

"No, no, it's not. I've been growing this for over eleven months! If I make it 'til next Saturday it will officially be a yeard."

"What the hell is a yeard?"

"It's when your beard is officially a year old," McMillan said and felt more than a little silly saying it.

Emma snorted back laughter and began to trot up the stairs, "Oh for fuck sake, does it get a birthday badge and cake?"

"No," McMillan whined quietly like a schoolboy and watched her ascending, "But me and the guys were going to have a few drinks to celebrate." He then noticed she hadn't got any pants on and momentarily forgot his own name.

Later, McMillan's thoughts tormented him as he lay seconds from slumber, shadowy figures looming in the dark corners of the room. Most of DeadBeard's victims, well the men, hadn't seen a thing; they had been lying in bed when they felt something sting them. A few moments later they fell back asleep, next to their partners and were awakened sometime later by the paramedics who had just kicked their door down.

Why did he do it?

Assuming DeadBeard was a he that is?

How did he get in and out undetected?

He rolled over and slid an arm around his snoring wife, a horrific image of her screaming as she woke up with the skin of his lower face stuck to her own with industrial strength superglue prevented sleep from giving him respite. The female victims were left permanently disfigured too, thick red scar tissue where the adhesive had been made them all look like they had beards of their own.

The men, the ones that hadn't died from shock or infection had to undergo skin grafts and God only knows what. DeadBeard wanted them to live, the always anonymous tip-off to the emergency services made sure of that. There was no connection between the people, other than the man's preference for facial hair. His own preference for facial hair.

Did he want to destroy these people's looks because he saw himself as a freak? Once again McMillan looked at his wife's beautiful sleeping face and made a vow that if he made his beard into a yeard, then he would shave and put himself and his wife out of danger. McMillan rolled over and switched off the bedside lamp, shifted his weight over to get comfortable, it was hot, so he flopped a leg over the duvet. He pushed out a colossal fart and settled down to attempt sleep.

3.

Kris clenched his teeth together and hooked out green speckles of broccoli trapped between the front two with a fingernail.

His head was freshly shaved and his grey-black beard groomed to perfection, a quick splash of cologne and he was ready.

Kris wore stereotypical garb for a college lecturer, even though he was in his mid-forties, he thought retro was always in fashion and he knew it had charmed at least one lady half his age.

Deborah Stewart, one of his students, the taboo love affair that was even more illicit due to the fact that he was married to a successful solicitor. She was a woman who could not be resisted, the affair, not the wife, young and voluptuous with skin like honey.

Kris didn't know what the hell she saw in him, and to be quite honest didn't really care, just as long as she was willing to show that golden honeyed body to him and let him get his wicked way. Kris lived for the moment, he saw no point in worrying about what ifs, and he would enjoy this little fling for however long he could get away with it.

The doorbell chimed and he marvelled at her impeccable timekeeping, it was such a rare trait nowadays. He whistled excitedly to himself, the wife was away for the weekend on the other side of the country, it would be the first time he and Deborah had the chance of spending the whole night together. Bliss. Kris unfastened door and let Deborah in, smiling at the black dress she had on.

She pounced on him within seconds of the doing being closed, fingers in his beard pulling, tongue in his mouth playing.

"Woh Nelly," Kris said, "What's got into you?"

Deborah grabbed him by the tie and pulled him in the direction of the bedroom with lustful glee, "It's what's going to get into me that I'm bothered about."

The romantic evening together Kris had planned with his student didn't exactly go as planned. Sex with Deborah was, as ever, amazing but it happening so suddenly when he had expected to wine and dine her kind of quelled the excitement of the evening, and it resulted in dinner being burnt.

Deborah didn't seem that bothered about the meal he had prepared and took it upon herself to order take away pizza. Kris wasn't too happy about his culinary efforts going to waste and even though he ate more than his fair share of the deep pan, he knew that the cheese would give him indigestion.

Kris grumbled quietly to himself and got out of the bed.

Deborah put a bare foot on his hairy buttock, "Don't be too long, I want round two."

Kris chuckled to her and strutted out of the bedroom to the en-suite bathroom. He took the indigestion tablets from the cabinet and pressed three out into his hand. He popped the fruit flavoured tablets in his mouth and crunched them quickly whilst he pissed in the toilet.

A quick hand-wash and back he went into the boudoir for the second course. The light from the en-suite bathroom lie across Deborah's nakedness, he stopped and admired the view for a few seconds.

"Ha, ha very funny," Kris said crossing the room, Deborah was still, her eyes closed and breathing through her nose heavily with the impression of sleep. Calling her bluff, Kris crept up to the bed and knelt on the bottom.

He lowered his face to her bare feet and blew gently. No reaction, she was definitely faking. Slowly he started to crawl on his hands and knees up and over her sprawled out naked body leaving a trail of kisses. Deborah kept the pretence up, even when he got level with her neatly trimmed pubes. Kris watched her breasts rise and fall, her face still passive, asleep. He smirked and touched the tip of his tongue against her vaginal lips. Still, she wouldn't move. Kris frowned and knelt beside her thinking that maybe she actually was asleep. Ah well, he thought, we have all weekend. He gently pulled the bedsheets over her, half expecting her to jump up and scare him at any point. Something passed across the rectangle of light coming from the en-suite, Kris spun round to feel a sharp scratch on his throat. A few seconds of horrified confusion washed over Kris's face as he toppled forwards towards his attacker. The tall, thin figure that stood there stepped back into the bathroom, hypodermic needle still clutched between its long spindly fingers and the last thought Kris had before he fell unconscious was *there's an alien in my en-suite.*

4.

The first one I did was this fat, disgustingly hairy college professor.

This guy looked as though his mother was a fucking gorilla for fuck sake. Thick, black hair all over him, his arse crack was like the Black Forest. His stupid beard was huge too, practically joined to his chest hair. People like this exist to rub it in the hairless faces of us follicly challenged alopeciacs.

I followed him around, got to know his routines and schedules, knew he was nailing some girl who he taught, like some filthy fucking pervert. I picked the lock on his back door whilst he was out; it had taken me a while to learn that particular trick. I found a suitable place to hide, beneath the only bed in the house and waited. I must have been under there for at least four hours, I heard them fucking.

It took him precisely thirty-two thrusts before he shot in her and I'm no expert, but she sounded like she was faking her enjoyment. When he came he made a weird mewling noise and then grunted like a pig. If I had not been worried that one of the bed springs was going to jut out and pop one of my eyeballs, perhaps I would have found their act of intimacy arousing, or his noises amusing.

And so I waited and waited for an opportunity to show itself.

He went to the toilet, after forty-five minutes of relentless bitching about indigestion, to take a piss and get medication and I made my move.

I slid out from under the bed without a sound. In one motion I clamped one hand across the woman's mouth and injected her with the secret concoction in the hypodermic.

I'm not going to tell you what I used; your medical professionals should have worked that one out by now.

She went wide-eyed for a couple of seconds before succumbing to the drugs.

I quickly turned myself around 180 degrees so my head was at the foot of the bed.

The professor naturally thought she was faking sleep; one doesn't usually ask for Chapter Two in the Karma Sutra and then fall asleep a minute later. So the kinky bastard starts doing stuff to her comatose body. I don't know exactly what, but it wouldn't have surprised me one iota if he had proceeded to screw her unconscious body.

I got impatient and slipped out from beneath the bed, my shadow fell over his kneeling body and he jumped and turned around.

A quick jab with the second hypo and he was snoring like an emphysemic boar.

Now they were both out of it, I could relax for a few minutes.

I stretched out and limbered up before going down to his kitchen for a drink of water and to retrieve my bag, which I had previously stowed in his outside bin.

I lay the pair of them side by side and pulled my scalping knife out of the bag. This thing was a work of art, an expensive replica of a Sioux Indian horn handle blade. I unsheathed it, this knife was so sharp it could circumcise a flea and went to work straight away.

I wanted to do a good job, skinning someone is a delicate procedure, you can't rush these things. I fucked up a bit around the mouth, a few bits where the tip of the knife poked through the skin where I didn't want it to, but overall I think I did alright.

There was a lot of blood, but not half as much as I thought there was going to be. Once I had loosened the beard and attached skin from his face, I peeled it off like a latex mask and laid it carefully on a pillow.

I yanked away one of the bed sheets and wrapped it around his head and face with his nose out so he didn't suffocate and rolled him over into the recovery position so he wouldn't choke on his own blood.

I didn't want the cunt to die; the whole point of this project is to make people suffer the shocked stares and averted eyes. I made sure I was quick, I pressed the beard mask firmly on to the pillow to remove as much of the excess blood as possible, then got my next tool from the bag.

Now, this stuff costs a fortune, UltraBond extra strength adhesive spray. It is rumoured to be the strongest adhesive in commercial use, get this on your skin and it'll leave permanent scarring.

But it sticks almost anything to anything.

I flipped the beard mask over and sprayed it with the UltraBond. You have to leave it for five seconds before sticking it to something, so I counted in my head. *One elephant. Two elephants.*

Three elephants. Four elephants. Five elephants. I carefully pressed the beard wig against the woman's face. As I expected, it was a little too big, but I made sure it fit perfectly around her mouth chin and jaw. I was happy once the whole beard area of her face was covered with her lover's facial area. It stuck firmly within ten seconds.

Once I was satisfied that I had done everything according to my plan, I picked up my things and left.

I rang the emergency services from the first phone box I passed, which I had previously located a few streets away.

5.

"Don't you ever worry that you're becoming a prissy pretentious faggot though?" Jonathan said picking at the corner of the label on his ale bottle.

His friend David stroked his beard gently like it was some resting bushy animal nesting on his face. He had spent over a year growing and cultivating his beard, tending to it daily with moisturising lotions, oils and combs specifically designed for facial topiary. He lifted a glass of thick, cloudy cider to his mouth, sipped it thoughtfully and said, "No."

Jonathan swigged his ale and tugged at his own lengthy beard, dark brown and streaked with a few grey lines. His mate David was fond of saying that his own grey hairs were earnt one for every ass he had kicked, Jonathan just thought his own was because he was old.

The beer garden was silent apart from some lanky hooded chav drinking Budweiser across the way. It was peaceful, the evening sunny with just the right amount of breeze to keep it bearable. Jonathan finished his bottle and stood up, his six and a half foot figure cast an ominous shadow, The Grim Reaper or something Frankenstein made out of metalheads. It never failed to impress David, who was almost a foot shorter than his friend and thick-set; he had first-hand experience of the arses Jonathan had kicked.

When they had met it had been in this pub, David thought he would act the hard man and approach the biggest baddest bastard in the joint and start something. Jonathan had acted like the gentle giant, batting away David's insults like mildly annoying flies with a bemused expression on his face whilst he continued his seduction of a curvy brunette.

Until David, in his ridiculous drunken state decided to insult the good lady, Jonathan had pounded the living shit out of him then.

Most normal people who had taken such an unbelievable brutal battering would have limped off with their tail tucked between their legs and licked their wounds. Most people wouldn't have dared venture back to the same guy in the same venue the week after. But David did. David knew he had been out of order, known he had been acting like a fly-infested monkey turd. There was no excuse for his behaviour that night and he wasn't going to waste his breath making one up, so he did the right thing. He went to the bar and bought Jonathan ale and put it in front of him. He apologised. He thanked him for beating the crap out of him, as the way he had been acting he was lucky it hadn't been worse. A kind of uneasy rapport grew into a firm friendship over the years, until they got to where they were now. Brothers in beard.

When Jonathan had vanished down the steps into the dark mouth of the pub, David gazed at the hooded figure sitting at the far table. The way he was hunched up inside his baggy clothes made him look skeletal, anorexic. David presumed he was an addict of some kind, dark circles beneath protruding eyes flitted this way and that with the erratic twitching of a paranoiac. His paper-thin mouth muttered to itself, inaudible to anyone but its owner. When the rolling eyes locked on to David's, David looked away.

"You." The hooded figure said, his voice was higher than he expected a nasal whine.

David pretended not to hear him, stared into his pint and fiddled with his phone.

A whisper of material and the skeletal man appeared beside him. "Hey man."

David turned, noticed the guy's hairless eyebrows beneath the hood made his piercing eyes all the sharper. David grumbled, "Alright?"

When the man smiled it was terrifying, a pink skeleton, more rictus than a grin. "You got a light?"

The man's breath reeked and even though David didn't smoke anymore, he always carried a lighter in case he got lucky enough to pull someone who did. With the intention of getting rid of the bloke as quick as possible, David got his disposable lighter and handed it to the skinny man. He plucked it from his hand with impossibly long fingers.

"Thanks, man." He said and fumbled in his coat pocket.

Jonathan flicked the sunglasses down from his forehead, picked up the freshly bought drinks and strode across the pub towards the beer garden.

A sudden noise, like a wildcat in pain, made the big man jump and the bottle of ale he was carrying slipped from his hand and exploded on the floor. "For fuck sake!" he said angrily at the wet patch of glass and beer on the ground when something came pinwheeling across the patio like Ghost Rider.

David ran towards him, his whole face in flames, the skin bubbling and boiling, his beard and moustache an effigy of fire. Jonathan did the first thing he could think of and threw the contents of the remaining drink in his friend's face.

The cider extinguished the flames, but David still ran blindly forwards and toppled down the flight of stone steps into the pub. Jonathan crouched down beside his shrieking friend and screamed out for help, even though David's blackened face made him think it was too late for that.

Somehow David was alive when the ambulance got to him. Somehow.

Jonathan was still in shock when he got back home. Two and a half hours sat in the pub talking to some big ginger detective had been a chore, when all he cared about was the welfare of his friend. The cop didn't verify whether they thought it was another DeadBeard attack. It was too soon, and for all anyone had known, the nutter that had been going around attacking bearded folk may have inspired a copycat.

Nevertheless, he had told the detective everything he had known, which wasn't much, just some druggie chav bloke in the beer garden who he hadn't paid hardly any attention to.

There was nothing else to say.

Jonathan hung the phone up, there was still no news on David's condition, and he was fobbed off with stereotypical phrases and told that they might know more the following day.

He collapsed into a threadbare armchair in front of the television, his head full of beer and fuzzy with fatigue. He stared at the blank flat screen and reached beside the armchair for the remote control.

His fingers brushed against skin and he leapt out of the chair just as a tall figure lunged at him with a hypodermic needle. The figure had been hiding behind the armchair, waiting for him to get comfortable before it attacked. Jonathan backed away from the freakish, naked man. He was at least the same height as him, something that didn't happen very often, and he was completely hairless, pale skinned.

"Get the fuck away from me," Jonathan said gearing himself up for a fight. Was this just some escaped mental patient?

The man smiled at Jonathan, a Grinch grin with more than a little of Tolkien's Golem. Lips that drew back too far over greying gums were blue-white lines, a natural clown with human makeup.

He ran across the room, with the needle poised ready, but luckily for Jonathan, he was not a stranger to fighting. He ducked the freak's flailing arms and jabbed him hard just below the ribs. The freak doubled over and Jonathan shoved him into his DVD cabinet, sending cases and discs everywhere.

He laid on the floor all arms and legs and just the man's frailty made Jonathan almost feel guilty for striking him. But that moment of guilt was soon washed away when the man shot out a bare foot attached to a long leg and kicked him squarely in the testicles.

Jonathan doubled over grabbing himself and hurried away from the man, who started to get to his feet. He shoulder barged the door open and half fell into the hallway. The man stumbled after him, grin still etched on his face, and needle still held high.

Jonathan righted himself and steadied himself against the wall. He knew he needed to take this bloke down, he just didn't want to get anywhere near that needle.

The hallway was bare except for a pointless umbrella stand that had been there for years, a red and black striped golfing umbrella, filthy and rusted, was the only thing it contained. Jonathan snatched at the handle and held it out like a sword as he backed away towards the front door.

Jonathan attempted to unlock the door blindly; he dared not take his eyes off the stalking man. He had just felt the cold of the metal key when the crazy man hurled himself at him. Jonathan braced himself for the attack, umbrella jutting out like a spear and stared dumbfounded at the slippery snake-like movements of his attacker.

The man swerved out of the way of the umbrella's rusted metal tip, dropped to the floor like his legs were made of rubber and sunk the needle into Jonathan's left thigh.

Whatever was in the syringe made his leg go numb.

He pitched over forwards towards the naked man as the numbness took over and he fell to the floor unconscious.

Intense searing agony brought him hurtling back to consciousness.

Something, or someone, thumping against the front door, blood running down his face, his t-shirt soaked. His flat screen television had the volume turned up high, and stuck smack bang in the centre of the screen was the skin and hair from the lower half of his face.

6.

I'll admit it; I should have stopped after the beard on the telly guy. He could have easily kicked the shit out of me if he hadn't been so worried about getting the needle in him. He saw me, yeah the others, well one or two, caught glimpses of me too, but this guy had more than enough time to somehow give the fuzz an accurate description of yours truly. I should have slit his throat. I regret that now. Within twenty-four hours of that attack, an artist's depiction of me was all over the TV and newspapers nationwide. I knew I wouldn't be able to get away with this shit for long, I am not stupid, but I wanted to go out with a bang. I wanted people to be talking about me, about DeadBeard for years to come.

I had been keeping an eye on the detective in charge of my investigation, it was as though the police were dangling the proverbial carrot in front of me, and a big bastard ginger bearded one and all. I was wary but thorough with my own investigation into this detective McMillan. I followed him, to my knowledge without his detection.

I found out all the necessary information I needed to make him my last victim.

It was whilst I was scoping out McMillan's place that I saw yet another bearded bastard, and even though I didn't want to jeopardise my plans for McMillan, I couldn't resist following him. I carried my bag with me most of the time; I was in a disguise - itchy blonde wig, glasses, hat and a moustache. It may be another impulsive attack, like the guy in the beer garden, but when I saw this twat I just couldn't fight the urge.

7.

Matt pulled the peak of his khaki cap over his eyes. He wished he had remembered his sunglasses, the reflective sparkle of sunlight bouncing off the passing cars burnt into his retinas. He paused, told Gremlin to stay, and stretched out his calf muscles. Gremlin was a yellow Labrador. The dog obeyed and stared up at his master as he did his stretching exercises.

Matt unzipped a pocket on his running top and swiped open his mobile phone and quickly thumbed out a text message. He's following me down Princes Street; I'm going to cut through the park.

He then opened up his running app and started the tracker. He casually turned his face, stretching his neck, and saw the tall man pretending to check the bus timetable on the opposite side of the road.

He had been walking up and down the town with Gremlin for the best part of two weeks, under constant surveillance by his colleagues. His house, well the one the police were using in this sting, was rigged out with all the latest in motion sensors and security equipment.

Now they had put out the artist impression of DeadBeard that they had managed to get a lot more information for from his last victim, they expected him to either strike again or vanish. The main thing, the main thing they were focusing on, was his apparent height. The last victim was six foot seven in his socks and he was sure that his attacker was taller than him. That couldn't be hidden easily. He could disguise himself with a variety of different styles, he could paint himself blue and dress up like Tinkerbell, but there was nothing he could do about his height.

The man who had been following him was at least seven foot tall. Beige slacks and a long-sleeved shirt, dark glasses and a baseball cap. A drooping blonde moustache that he kept scratching at, irritated his face, and every time he adjusted his cap, his hair moved unnaturally. Matt was certain that this was the man. He had stopped somewhere crowded to stretch, make it appear he was about to run with his dog. He text his colleagues to tell them of his plan and saw their reply pop up at the top of the screen as he started the running app. Matt squatted down and petted Gremlin's head, "ready boy?"

Matt jogged at a steady pace, not too quick not too slow. As he approached the entrance to the park, he checked in the reflections of buildings and parked cars to make sure his stalker was keeping up. Sure enough, the bloke had crossed over the road and was hurrying after him, a determined expression on his face.

Matt reduced his speed as he passed through the iron gates and into the park, Gremlin trotting beside him happily. The park was small, just a grassed over area with a few trees in the middle of the town, hardly a park really but it was still referred to as one. He took the winding path through the trees, subtly checking the man was following him.

"Oi," Matt heard the man shouting after him and it took him by surprise. It was unusual for them to be so open. The man's voice boomed across the park. Matt continued to jog a bit further whilst he contemplated what to do.

The man shouted out to him again and this time there was no hiding the fact he had noticed him. Matt stopped and leaned up against the wall of the public toilets, pretended to stretch again while the man strode purposefully towards him.

Matt peered across to the other side of the park to where his colleagues should be sat in an unmarked vehicle. The road was obscured by the trees but he had absolute faith that they would be where they were supposed to be.

"Oi, you!" The tall man marched up to him, face red from sudden exertion.

Matt took a deep breath, readying himself for physical confrontation.

The man was a lot older than he imagined.

He held something out towards Matt making him instinctively flinch until he saw what it was. A black dog bag.

"Yours I believe." The tall man said sternly thrusting the tied black bag at him. "If you are going to go to the effort of cleaning up after your dog, then at least take it with you and dispose of it properly rather than just leaving it on the high street."

Matt frowned for a few seconds before he remembered Gremlin doing an epic shit by the bus stop just before he decided to go through the park. He had bagged it up and that was when he noticed the tall guy. He now remembered putting the bag on the bus shelter's plastic seat and not retrieving it.

"Shit," Matt muttered ashamed of himself and reached for the bag.

"Yes, quite." The man said and dropped the bag into Matt's hand before about turning on the spot like a soldier and marching off back the way he had come.

Matt leaned against the wall of the toilet and watched the man stride out of the park with a spring in his step, happy to have done a good thing.

"Well," Matt said smiling down at Gremlin who had decided to take a moment to lie down in the sun, "I feel like a total prick now. Come on." He tugged on the dog lead just as a hand appeared from the entrance to the public toilets and clamped over his mouth as its owner pounced out of the shadows and injected something into his throat.

A tall man dressed in denim, a trucker's cap, long ginger hair, matching moustache, smiled a jack o' lantern grin at him as he slowly slumped down next to the comatose dog.

"You said you felt like a prick." The tall man in the denim said in his whiny voice and laughed a wheezing laugh.

Two people sat in the twenty-year-old Ford Sierra, rusted patches covered its blue painted bodywork like freckles on a Smurf. Nev Murray ran a hand over the stubble of his scalp and grimaced. Sitting for long periods made his back hurt, he wanted out.

"Come on for fuck sake, let's just go and have a look." He said leaning his head towards his partner.

Jo Harwood rolled her eyes and checked her mobile phone for the fiftieth time. Still no message from Matt. "I don't want to ruin anything. He's the one in charge of this thing."

Nev sighed, "Yeah but it's been at least half an hour. Check his GPS."

Jo tapped a series of buttons on the phone's screen; a little blue dot showed her where Matt was. "He's still in the park."

Nev snatched the keys from the car's ignition and pushed his sunglasses on, "Fuck it, let's go check."

Jo could hardly argue with her superior, so even though she thought they should wait until Matt signalled them, she followed her partner.

They walked down the street like a pair of badass American homicide detectives. Nev always imagined himself as the British version of Die Hard's John McClane; he certainly had the haircut for it.

Jo was sultry enough and had the sex appeal of the man-eating detective, not to mention the colourful language, like Dexter Morgan's hot sister Deborah in the series about the Miami vigilante.

The street wasn't particularly quiet, the usual hustle and bustle for a weekday lunchtime, and even though Nev was prepared to kick some serious arse, a rumble in his tummy told him that he was equally prepared to murder a burrito. That's what the cool American cops ate in the programmes, especially the ones where the sun was always blazing. It wasn't until six months ago that he realised a burrito wasn't one of those wide-brimmed Mexican hats. Images of him halfway through eating a burrito, with the works, and spotting a perp, hurling the food into the nearest bin before pelting down the street like Mel Gibson in one of the Lethal Weapon films, one or two probably, they were too old for running in the last ones.

Jesus if they made any more they would need Zimmers and wheelchairs.

They walked into the park, Jo playing by the rules and radioing in their whereabouts and plan. The park was quite busy, business people grabbing a quick respite amongst the trees, grass and flowers. Couples walking dogs, students lounging on the grass casually in groups. Then an ear piercing screech broke out from the centre of the park and all heads span in that direction. Nev and Jo looked at one another before instinctively running towards the source of the noise.

Nev was fast but Jo was quicker, and as he watched her race around a bend in the path, he saw her freeze and her hands fly to her face. He pushed himself harder, his heart pounding; a woman crossed his path with a baby stroller.

I'm gonna jump it; I'm gonna fucking jump it!

His inner badass shouted as he neared the panicking mother.

But just as he was about to make what would be a rather embarrassing and painful for all parties involved, attempt at leaping over the baby stroller, he remembered he wasn't John McClane, and that he was pushing fifty with a bad back.

Nev swerved out of the way of the terrified mother, nearly fell over a litter bin and finally caught up with Jo. There was a circle of people by the public toilets, a few women comforting another who was in obvious distress, whilst another few were crouched by and holding down something on the grass.

For a few seconds they didn't know what it was, sand coloured and rolling in the grass, but then Jo muttered, "It's Gremlin."

The dog made horrific whining yowls as it feebly pawed at its face. Matt, the undercover police officer's skinned beard was glued to its face haphazardly.

"The sick, sick cunt," Nev said outraged and headed for the public toilets. "Jo," he pointed to the crowd and distraught Labrador, "can you sort this?"

She nodded and started radioing for help as he entered the toilets.

The floor was drenched. Blood mixed with piss and God only knew what, these toilets were never clean for long. A pair of feet stuck out from beneath the only cubicle in there, a ginger wig lay between them wet with blood.

Nev fished in his trousers pocket for a coin and slid it into the groove in the lock on the door.

Matt lay against the filthy porcelain toilet, the skin of his lower face torn off and a deep gash in his throat.

DeadBeard had upped his game, he was killing them now.

8.

McMillan stared at himself in the mirror, the circles that had started out as light grey smudges beneath his eyes were becoming darker as the days went by. They were no closer to catching DeadBeard, and now he had lost one of his best men due to the psychopath.

Throat slit in a stinking park toilets, in broad fucking daylight, and yet still nobody had seen the bastard.

The latest attack had got the hairs up on the animal activists' backs too now, that poor bloody dog. The vets had done everything they could to ease its suffering but the fumes from the extra strength super glue had been even more harmful to its lungs than it would a human.

Didn't this sick bastard like anything?

Was nothing beyond his wrath?

McMillan brought the electric razor up towards his face, now that DeadBeard had started deliberately killing; Emma had become even more frantic about him getting rid of his pride and joy.

He pulled at the long ginger hair on his chin; it would be a year old in less than twenty-four hours. Did a bunch of wiry hairs really mean that much to him? Was it really worth putting himself and his wife, at risk just for some stupid facial hair phase he was going through?

McMillan rolled his thumb across the ON/OFF switch, took a deep breath and brought the buzzing razor towards his 364-day growth. His stomach squirmed; his heart throbbed as the whirring blades sawed back and forth at an alarming rate, closer and closer to his beard.

When his phone burst into life and began to dance on the bathroom shelf he jumped and dropped the razor into the sink with a loud clatter. He switched it off and picked up his phone, it was Chris, his best mate, his brother in the journey of epic beard growth. Every time he got a phone call recently from one of his friends who had been harnessing their inner Viking, he expected the worst. Despite their bravado and determination not to bow to the threat of some weird beard hating psychopath, he wouldn't blame them for getting rid of the facial hair, it was better than the alternative.

He answered the phone.

"Hey dude, just checking that you're still on for tomorrow night man?" Chris said excitedly, not giving him time to confirm or deny anything.

"The guys and I are so damn proud of you man and guess what? Your page, Badass Bearded Nation has now reached 5k followers. There are people coming from all over the country to your Yeard party tomorrow."

"Woh Chris slow down a minute," McMillan said trying to get a word in edgeways with his babbling friend.

"No, wait, that's not the best of it. A local biker chapter, The Wasters are coming to provide security. They think you're a hero man."

McMillan was dumbstruck by all the information he had to process. This DeadBeard dude had made him even more infamous. His little community page on Facebook had escalated rapidly since the DeadBeard attacks, trebled in size. Five thousand people. How could he let all those people down? He stared into the mirror with grim determination.

Just one more day.

"Okay, I'll be there." He said to his best friend.

Just one more day.

McMillan tidied the bathroom up, slapped on his favourite beard oil and walked out of the room.

A low desperate moan escaped from his throat as he saw Emma standing in front of him, the thin but muscular arm of an incredibly tall man wrapped around her neck. He was painted red with strange white symbols streaked onto his body to accentuate different parts. A white strip crossed his intense bulging eyes. He held a weird looking knife against Emma's forehead, a red mark where the blade had sliced into the skin just below her hairline.

An elaborate Native American feathered headdress was tied to his head, the top of it bending against the ceiling.

"Hello pig, we meet at last," DeadBeard said in his whiny voice with a grin that seemed too big for his face.

Even though she was petrified, apart from the small cut on her forehead, Emma looked unharmed. McMillan could see the dark red marks beneath her chin where DeadBeard's paint was rubbing.

"Please, don't hurt her." McMillan shrieked.

"Please." He added again, pleading with the man.

DeadBeard laughed and passed the knife he held to the hand around Emma's throat.

He reached down to the leather loincloth he was wearing; he pulled out an identical knife with the handle of an animal horn. "You know the score copper." He threw the knife at McMillan's feet and reached behind himself to delve into a small leather satchel that was tied across one shoulder. He shook the large can of adhesive before dropping it to the floor. "This time though, you get to do all the work yourself. Or I scalp this whole."

McMillan shot a glance at his wife and the knife pressed against her pretty throat. Her beautiful flawless skin would be ruined; he had seen the effects that the glue had on his other victims faces, the red raw scarring. Like their very own scar beard. But they could live with that, he loved her no matter what.

DeadBeard moved his knife into his other hand and held the blade against Emma's forehead once more; his other hand plucked a strand of her long red hair. Her long red hair.

Her long red fake hair.

A recent trend that a few young women had gotten into of late was to have their natural hair cropped really short and wear wigs. Emma herself had done a total head shave for charity three months previous. Whilst the hair grew back slowly, she liked the novelty of wearing different coloured wigs; they fit well with her slightly alternative appearance. She had names for all of the half dozen she owned. The white one was Storm, the pink Barbarella, and the red one was after The Little Mermaid.

She was wearing the Ariel one.

McMillan caught her eye as he crouched down and picked the knife up at his feet. He hoped and prayed that she would understand what he was about to do, it was her joke after all. McMillan started to stand up slowly, all the while keeping eye contact with Emma.

Now or never, he thought, trying his best to telepathically communicate his intentions to her. One word was all he said, simply, "Quack."

The few seconds that passed before the realisation hit Emma seemed to take forever, and then she went wide-eyed and dropped to the floor. Sudden confusion appeared on DeadBeard's face as he was left with just an expensive wig in one hand and a traditional Native American scalping knife in the other.

McMillan jumped up slamming his left hand into DeadBeard's wrist, knocking the knife to the floor, the right hand holding the other knife into the side of his red painted belly, and his forehead hard onto the bridge of his nose.

The tall scrawny man dropped to the floor unconscious, nose broken and a knife in his side. It wouldn't be fatal, McMillan was sure of that, but it would give the cunt something to remember him by.

Emma dived into his arms and they risked a five-second embrace before McMillan told her to call for help whilst he restrained DeadBeard. Emma sniffed back her snot and tears and scowled down at the near-naked red man who tried to harm her husband and her. "Just a minute."

Police covered everywhere, a paramedic led McMillan and his wife to an ambulance where she could have the cut on her head seen to.

A stretcher was wheeled out with the now conscious DeadBeard wailing and shrieking obscenities and promises of revenge at McMillan.

Several police officers accompanied the stretcher just in case he broke free of his restraints. They didn't need to use handcuffs but had clamped them around his red wrists as a preventative. The fact that the palm of each hand was glued to the sides of his face and jaw like he was permanently screaming seemed restraining enough.

McMillan thought about the permanent scarring that the glue would make and visualised the hand shaped red welts that would disfigure the sick bastard for the rest of his life and smiled.

The End.

Author Biography

Matthew Cash, or Matty-Bob Cash as he is known to most, was born and raised in in Suffolk; which is the setting for his debut novel Pinprick. He is compiler and editor of Death By Chocolate, a chocoholic horror Anthology, Sparks, the 12Days: STOCKING FILLERS Anthology, and its subsequent yearly annuals and has numerous releases on Kindle and several collections in paperback.

In 2016 he started his own label Burdizzo Books, with the intention of compiling and releasing charity anthologies a few times a year. He is currently working on numerous projects, his second novel FUR will hopefully be launched 2018.

He has always written stories since he first learnt to write and most, although not all tend to slip into the many layered murky depths of the Horror genre.

His influences ranged from when he first started reading to Present day are, to name but a small select few;

Roald Dahl, James Herbert, Clive Barker, Stephen King, Stephen Laws, and more recently he enjoys Adam Nevill, F.R Tallis, Michael Bray, Gary Fry, William Meikle and Iain Rob Wright (who featured Matty-Bob in his famous A-Z of Horror title M is For Matty-Bob, plus Matthew wrote his own version of events which was included as a bonus).

He is a father of two, a husband of one and a zoo keeper of numerous fur babies.

You can find him here:

www.facebook.com/pinprickbymatthewcash

https://www.amazon.co.uk/-/e/B010MQTWKK

Other Releases By Matthew Cash

Novels

Virgin And The Hunter

Pinprick

FUR

Novellas

Ankle Biters

KrackerJack

Illness

Clinton Reed's FAT

Hell And Sebastian

Waiting For Godfrey

Deadbeard

The Cat Came Back

Krackerjack 2

Werwolf

Short Stories

Why Can't I Be You?

Slugs And Snails And Puppydog Tails

OldTimers

Hunt The C*nt

Anthologies Compiled and Edited By Matthew Cash

Death By Chocolate

12 Days: STOCKING FILLERS

12 Days: 2016 Anthology

12 Days: 2017 [with Em Dehaney]

The Reverend Burdizzo's Hymn Book (with Em Dehaney)

Sparks [with Em Dehaney]

Anthologies Featuring Matthew Cash

Rejected For Content 3: Vicious Vengeance

JEApers Creepers

Full Moon Slaughter

Down The Rabbit Hole: Tales of Insanity

Collections

The Cash Compendium Volume 1

Website:

www.Facebook.com/pinprickbymatthewcash

PINPRICK
MATTHEW CASH

All villages have their secrets Brantham is no different.

Twenty years ago after foolish risk taking turned into tragedy Shane left the rural community under a cloud of suspicion and rumour.

Events from that night remained unexplained, memories erased, questions unanswered.

Now a notorious politician, he returns to his birthplace when the offer from a property developer is too good to decline.

With big plans to haul Brantham into the 21st century, the developers have already made a devastating impact on the once quaint village.

But then the headaches begin, followed by the nightmarish visions.

Soon Shane wishes he had never returned as Brantham reveals its ugly secret.

VIRGIN AND THE HUNTER
MATTHEW CASH

Hi I'm God. And I have a confession to make.

I live with my two best friends and the girl of my dreams, Persephone.

When the opportunity knocks we are usually down the pub having a few drinks, or we'll hang out in Christchurch Park until it gets dark then go home to do college stuff. Even though I struggle a bit financially life is good, carefree.

Well they were.

Things have started going downhill recently, from the moment I started killing people.

KRACKERJACK
MATTHEW CASH

Five people wake up in a warehouse, bound to chairs.

Before each of them, tacked to the wall are their witness testimonies.

They each played a part in labelling one of Britain's most loved family entertainers a paedophile and sex offender.

Clearly revenge is the reason they have been brought here, but the man they accused is supposed to be dead.

Opportunity knocks and Diddy Dave Diamond has one last game show to host and it's a knock out.

KRACKERJACK2
MATTHEW CASH

Ever wondered what would happen if a celebrity faked their own death and decided they had changed their minds?

Two years ago publicly shunned comedian Diddy Dave Diamond convinced the nation that he was dead only to return from beyond the grave to seek retribution on those who ruined his career and tainted his legacy.

Innocent or not only one person survived Diddy Dave Diamond's last ever game show, but the forfeit prize was imprisonment for similar alleged crimes.

Prison is not kind to inmates with those type of convictions and as the sole survivor finds out, but there's a sudden glimmer of hope.

Someone has surfaced in the public eye claiming to be the dead comedian.

FUR
MATTHEW CASH

The old aged pensioners of Boxford are very set in their ways, loyal to each other and their daily routines. With families and loved ones either moved on to pastures new or maybe even the next life, these folk can get dependant on one another.

But what happens when the natural ailments of old age begin to take their toll?

What if they were given the opportunity to heal and overcome the things that make every day life less tolerable?

What if they were given this ability without their consent?

When a group of local thugs attack the village's wealthy Victor Krauss they unwittingly create a maelstrom of events that not only could destroy their home, but everyone in and around it.

Are the old folk the cause or the cure of the horrors?

COMING SOON
FROM
BURDIZZO BOOKS

THE CHILDREN AT THE BOTTOM OF THE GARDDEN
JONATHAN BUTCHER

At the edge of the coastal city of Seadon there stands a dilapidated farmhouse, and at the back of the farmhouse there is a crowd of rotten trees, where something titters and calls.

The Gardden.

Its playful voice promises games, magic, wonders, lies – and roaring torrents of blood.

It speaks not just to its eccentric keeper, Thomas, but also to the outcasts and deviants from Seadon's criminal underworld.

At first they are too distracted by their own tangled mistakes and violent lives to notice, but one by one they'll come: a restless Goth, a cheating waster, a sullen concubine, a perverted drug baron, and a murderous sociopath.

Haunted by shadowed things with coal-black eyes, something malicious and ancient will lure them ever closer. And on a summer's day not long from now, they'll gather beneath the leaves in a place where nightmares become flesh, secrets rise up from the dark, and a voice coaxes them to play and stay, yes yes yes, forever.

Printed in Great Britain
by Amazon